Jonathan!

CF

For Amelia. PC

This edition first published in 2020
by New Frontier Publishing Europe Ltd.
Uncommon, 126 New King's Rd, London SW6 4LZ
www.newfrontierpublishing.co.uk

ISBN: 978-1-913639-27-3

Printed in China
10 9 8 7 6 5 4 3 2 1

Jonathan!

PETER CARNAVAS

illustrated by
Amanda Francey

Jonathan's father was sweeping the floor

when all of a sudden ...

'Not scary, Jonathan.'

Jonathan's sister was having a nap

when all of a sudden ...

SNAP!

'Not scary, Jonathan.'

Jonathan's mother was hanging the towels

when all of a sudden ...

GROWL!

'Not scary, Jonathan.'

So Jonathan walked away,

slowly,

until ...

he found himself climbing a bumpy green hill.

Then all of a sudden ... he wasn't quite sure ...

that bumpy green hill was a ..

DINOSAUR!

Jonathan took the beast back to his house.

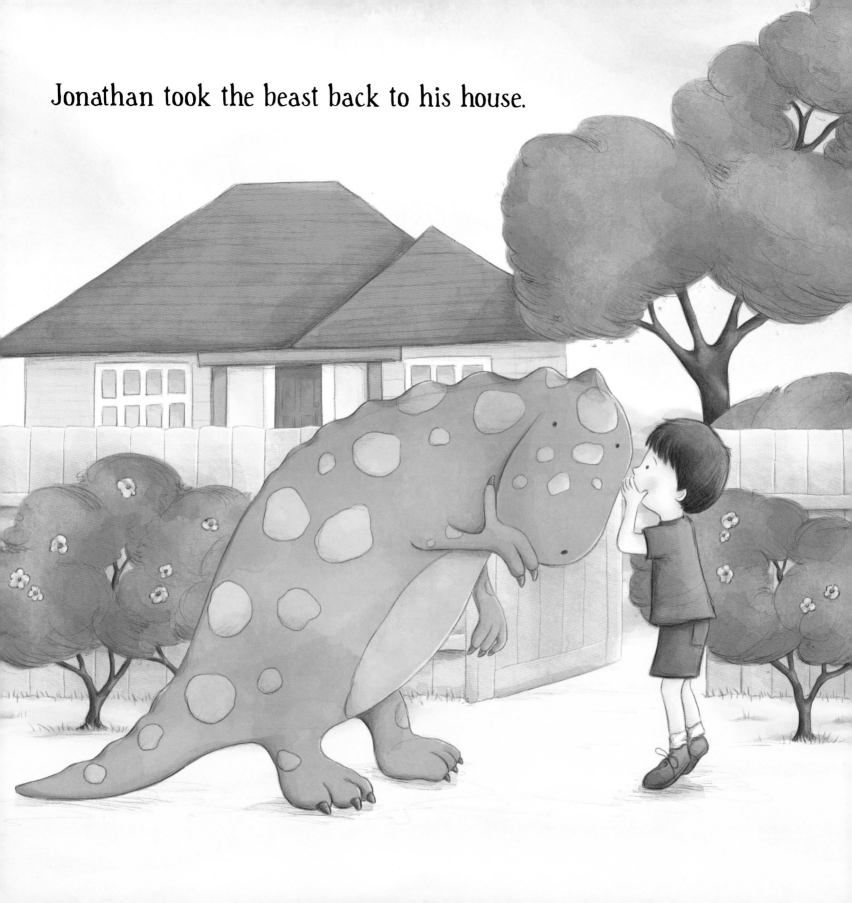

shhh!

They crept down the driveway, soft as a mouse.

Jonathan grinned.

Jonathan knocked.

Ever so slowly, the door was unlocked ...

BOO!

The family screamed!

The family fled!

'TOO SCARY, Jonathan!'
one of them said.

'Thank you,' said Jonathan. 'You can leave too.'

When all of a sudden ...

BOO!

'Not scary, Grandad.'